Little Doggie Stories

by

Marty Nemko

Aug 6, 2024

Hi Linda,
enjoy!

Marty Nemko

6th printing, revised

Praise for Marty Nemko

"Delectable bite-sized, short stories…It's difficult to stop reading them." Dr. Mark Goulston, author of *Just Listen.*

"Some unusual subjects to say the least! I highly recommend this worthwhile read." Michael Edelstein, author of *Three-Minute Therapy.*

"One of the few truly original thinkers of our time." Kathryn Riggs, retired, U.C. Berkeley School of Education."

"A really smart person." Michael Scriven, former president, American Evaluation Association.

"Magnificent food for thought." Walter Block, Wirth Eminent Scholar, Loyola U.

"The best of the best." Warren Farrell, author, *The Myth of Male Power.*

Marty Nemko

Photo credit: own work

- "Coach extraordinaire." *U.S. News*
- Author of 32 books, from *Careers for Dummies* to *Light: short-short stories of life's brighter side.*
- Ph.D., educational psychology, University of California Berkeley.
- Enjoys giving talks, being interviewed, and playing with his sweet doggie, Hachi.

To people who are kind to dogs.

A Note from the Author

Dear Reader,

I welcome your honest review of this book on Amazon as well as your email. I promise to respond. My email address is mnemko@comcast.net

Marty Nemko

Contents

SHORT-SHORT FICTIONAL STORIES

A Dog Named Yes and a Dog Named No

Hi, my name is Yes, and I used to be a cute dog but now, having roamed the streets of Oakland for five months, I'm matted and infected all over with foxtails. I'm a mess.

My doggie, Hachi. Own work

I don't blame my owners for having dumped me. I couldn't stop chewing their slippers, their sofa leg, even their electric toothbrush. So, this is my lot in life.

Or so I thought. Then I met a dog I call, No. I do that for a good reason. I'm a positive doggie and don't like to be critical. Every other dog I met was nice, but No? Everything was black.

I mean, we even saw this great bone — It must have been a barbecued rib! I toddled to pick it up and No said, "It could be rancid, even poisoned. Don't."

I figured the chances were great that the bone was just fine and the person just wasn't civic-minded and so tossed it on the street. I started chewing as No cringed. His loss — It was wonderful!

Then a truck pulled up. I had seen lots of trucks before — Beer trucks, sausage trucks, but this one had a sign I didn't understand: "Animal Control."

A man and a woman got out of the truck, came up to me and I was sure they wanted to pet me, but No screamed, "Run away. They're going to trap you, take you to the pound, and kill you!"

I didn't believe it but this time, No was right. The woman slipped this metal thing around my neck, pulled it tight and threw me into the back of the truck. No started to run away but the man got him too!

I was scared and No was terrified. And we got even more scared when we got to this gray building — It didn't look friendly. When we got inside, there were lots of dogs in CAGES, barking, whining, yelping. Was No right — Will we all get killed?

The woman threw us both into the same cage. We saw three other dogs in next cage and that made me feel good. At least we weren't the only doggies there.

The next day, we saw that one of the dogs, was gone. No said, "See?!"

And the day after, another dog was gone. But the one with a nice terrier was still there.

Later that day, the woman walked by with a man. He looked at us and I put my paws on the front of the cage and wagged my tail, and he said, "May I look at her?" But No growled and the man said, "Never mind. May I look at that terrier?"

The terrier wagged her tail and looked up at the man. And the man asked, "May I take her for a test walk?" The woman nodded, put the terrier on a leash, and they were off. I didn't see them again. So I'm guessing she got adopted. No said,

"I'm sorry I growled." I showed him that I forgave him by licking his face.

Two days later, even I was getting very scared that we might get killed. But a nice couple walked by. Again, I put my paws on the front of the cage and wagged my tail as wildly as I could. And this time, No stayed quiet. The woman pointed to me and said, "That dog seems nice."

And the woman opened the door — I was so happy, so happy — and nuzzled against his leg and then his wife's. He cried, looked at his wife who nodded, and she said, "Sweet doggie, you now have your forever home." I was so happy — but what about No?

Part of me wanted to stay with No — He needs a Yes, but I couldn't resist having a new home, maybe a forever home. So I toddled over to No, lifted my paw onto his face, kissed him, and said goodbye.

Church Dog

I thought I'd finally get some peace in my last assignment —Our Lady of the Plains church in Yorkshire. Hmmph.

Araujo Manuel, pxhere, CC0

The church, especially the Catholic Church, is about tradition, an anchor amid the roiling tides. So you can imagine how I felt when the following occurred.

It was just before I was to begin Midnight Mass on Christmas Eve no less, when, for once, we had a full house — I don't like that term, it evokes poker.

Just then, a woman who I had seen in the village with her dog but never in church — marched in with the dog — You'd think she'd feel more propriety. It was God knows what breed, probably no breed. It certainly had no Yorkshire Terrier in him, probably some random mix — whoever was around to, well, and forgive my language Lord, hump.

The last thing I wanted to do was chastise a parishioner, let alone just before starting Midnight Mass, so I just cleared my throat while staring at her for a moment, but it didn't work. She just sat down, with the dog on the aisle, no less!

Then just as I was about to start — as is the tradition — reciting the special proclamation of Jesus' birth, she stood up! And she lectured ME!

> Reverend Dunworthy, you know that Christianity is about accepting all. And many saints, not just Francis, not only accepted but venerated animals: St. Philip was unwilling to eat bird and became the saint of veganism. St. Cuthbert was the patron saint of, for God's sake, otters. And St. Gertrude, a woman I might add, is the patron saint of cats. And Reverend Dunworthy, do you not know the name of this church before the parishioners decided to change it to Our Lady of the Plains? St. Roche's Church. Do you know who St.

> Roche was? The patron saint of dogs! This very church was named after the patron saint of dogs!

The congregation twittered; a few even guffawed! I tried citing scripture, Philippians 3:2. "Watch out for those dogs, those evildoers, those mutilators of the flesh." But a congregant hissed. Hissed!

After the service, while I wanted to hide, I tried to maintain my churchy demeanor and stood at the door wearing my well-practiced beatific smile. Some of the congregants were polite, most escaped, and a few chastised me, of course, in an oh-so-Christian way, for example, "Father, do you think that just perhaps the church just might change just a wee bit with the times — even though we are in the Yorkshire Plains?"

As soon as Christianly possible, I escaped to the vestry and started to think about what to say next Sunday. I decided to say nothing — The problem would probably go away by itself.

Was I wrong! The next Sunday, not only did the woman bring her dog again, ten other people brought their dogs! As bad, even though it was now just another Sunday so the church was half empty, rather than parishioners taking seats in largely empty rows, nearly everyone chose to sit next to a dog! And during the service, instead of paying attention to my sermon, they were looking at a dog, petting a dog, even whispering to a dog!

What could I do? I stopped my sermon, walked down from the altar to the pews, brought a small dog up and said, "I guess the church must change with the times — even here in the Yorkshire Plains."

And I heard something I had never heard before in any church: the congregation cheered.

Can an Old Dog Learn a New Trick?

Rick Cameron, Flickr, CC 2.0

Starting way back when I was a puppy, my owner, Bill, tried to teach me to fetch. I would go after the tennis ball but it was in my genes to stay where the ball is and not bring it back. You see, over the millennia, hunters bred dogs for sense of smell, so the dogs could smell the poor animal that the hunter shot far away, go to the spot and wait, so the hunter could easily find his damn trophy.

I love Bill and so I want to please him. I knew he wanted me to bring the ball back when he kept saying, "Bring it back, bring it back, Buddy!" But it's hard, very hard, to triumph over your genes.

But then there was today. We were at the field and, as usual, Bill tossed the ball, closer than in years past because I can't run as far. Actually, I can't run at all —

waddle is more like it. He said his usual, "Bring it back, Buddy," not because he thought I would — It was just a habit, somehow comforting, I think to both of us.

But this time, something happened. I'm old now and maybe it's that I've become too tired to follow my genetic predisposition. Or maybe it's that over the years, my love for Bill has gotten so deep that it trumps the genes.

So, when I got to the ball, as usual, I started to lie down with it but when Bill said, "Bring it back, boy" I forced myself to put it in my mouth and took a step toward him.

Bill exclaimed, "Good, Buddy. Good Buddy!" That made me take another step, a faster one. Again, he exclaimed, "Good Buddy, the best Buddy!" And I actually started to trot, and made it all the way to him, where I dropped the ball at his feet and, because I was tired, I also dropped at his feet.

He cried. I cried. I love Bill and he loves me. Forever.

Who says you can't teach an old dog a new trick?

Dog Stolen. Reward.

FreePix,CC

Jessica had a stressful job as a social worker. So, more even than most dog owners, she was glad at the end of the day to get that fervent greeting from her sweet doggie, Bella.

Bella had to hold it in all day because Jessica lived in an apartment. So Jessica's first priority was to take Bella for a walk and, to kill two birds with one stone, they made a quick stop at Trader Joe's — She only needed half-and-half for her beloved morning coffee and spring greens for her daily, virtuous salad.

As usual, Jessica tied Bella to a post in an inconspicuous place on the side of Trader Joe's. For years, there was never a problem, but today when Jessica returned, Bella was gone.

Jessica raced around, drove around, yelling "Bella!" to no avail. She constantly checked her cell because Bella's tag listed her phone number…and the word "Reward."

Finally, adrenaline dissipated, Jessica plodded back home and got herself a glass of wine to wait out the vigil. "The damn thief will call to get his fucking reward."

And the thief did. Teresa, 18, single mother of two, struggling to live amid the noise of an SRO, felt desperate. So when she saw the docile Bella and the tag saying "Reward," Teresa took Bella who, trusting sweetie, came willingly.

Teresa said, "I've got your dog. I need $500."

Jessica, so relieved, suppressed anger and quickly said "Okay."

Teresa responded, "You answered too fast. A thousand, take it or leave it. I can get 2 for it."

Jessica, now educated, feigned tears, waited, and murmured, "That will wipe me out but…okay. Where should we meet?"

They met in a remote warehouse district, with Bella in Teresa's arms.

Jessica tearfully ran to Bella.

"Not so fast. We forgot about the $300 sales tax. $1,300 or I sell her."

Jessica, suppressing anger said, "Honestly, I don't have it. I took the $1,000 from the bank."

"Go to the ATM."

Jessica returned with the extra $300 and counted out $1,300 whereupon Teresa took the money and handed Bella back to Jessica.

Teresa laughed, "I would have taken 50 bucks. Maybe I should take up poker."

Second Love

Hachi, own work

I was retiring — People don't want a 75-year-old dentist. Sometimes, I wonder who my patients will miss more — me or Naomi my tiny, furry dirigible that sat on patients' laps while I was drilling, pulling, root-canaling.

Naomi too was at retirement age. She was 17. As I sat home on my first day of retirement, Naomi on my lap, I felt bad for her. She always had the stimulation of a parade of patients. Now she was stuck with just me. Should I get another dog? Am I too old? And with Naomi 17, maybe it would be good to have a young dog to ease my grief when Naomi goes.

That held sway and I signed up for alerts from PetFinder.com, AdoptaPet.com, and PetSmartCharities.org, which aggregate listings of available dogs from many shelters.

Mainly there were pit bulls and chihuahuas, not my type. But finally, a sweet little puffball named Angel came available. When I took Angel for the test walk, I introduced her to Naomi and it was love at first sight. And in the car, Naomi somehow knew that Angel wanted to be on my lap, so Naomi just curled up on the passenger seat. I lifted Angel onto my lap and she rested her head on my thigh as though we'd done that for years.

The three of us did great. Angel would run around Naomi to get her to play and for a while she did. But then, Naomi slowed further and even when Angel would paw at her to play, Naomi would barely raise her head, and then not even that. And then Naomi lost continence.

I took Naomi to the vet. Of course, Angel came with us — Angel, like Naomi, came everywhere with me. Before leaving the car, I hugged Angel for my benefit more than hers, and went in. The vet had that sad look when I asked, "Naomi is 18. Is it time?" She nodded and asked if I wanted to stay in the room. I did — I wanted her last moments to be with me.

The vet gently gave the injection and the already sleepy Naomi went to her final sleep. Then the vet asked if I'd like to stay in the room a while. She left, I cried and found myself pounding the wall in agony. Finally, when I got just a bit of control, I padded out into the waiting room, still teary.

A woman who had just left the other exam room with her puppy intuited what happened and hugged me. I don't know if it was my vulnerability but I stayed for a few moments in her arms, my head on her shoulders.

Then she lifted my head, we looked into each other's eyes, and she did the last thing I thought she would. She asked, "Would you like to go out for coffee?" And that's how she, her dog Sweetheart, my dog Angel, and I started dating.

Kisser

Liz West, Flickr, CC 2.0

The doorbell rang at 3 AM. I opened the door to find a wicker basket. In it wrapped in a blanket, was a puppy.

I work full-time. Who has time for a dog? Even if I got a dog sitter — That's expensive, and then there are the nights and weekends.

And the training! Who has time? Who wants pee and poop in the house?

So cute as the puppy was, I steeled myself, carried him into the car and drove to the pound.

She would not get off my lap. Indeed, the more I drove, the more she curled up. And then she fell asleep.

I was not going to have a dog!

I pulled into the pound's parking lot, saw the entrance — It reminded me of Auschwitz. I pursed my lips and lifted the puppy with one hand and started to reach for the car door with the other. And then, damn it, she licked my face.

I just couldn't do it. I closed the car door, yeah with the puppy and me inside. I named her based on what just happened. My forever companion would be named Kisser.

But if it was one thing I wouldn't let Kisser do is disrupt my sleep. So even before I got home, I went to the pet store and got a crate and a cushion to put inside it. Add the food, collar and leash, and tax and I was out $247. And that was before the vet visit. Perfectly healthy but needing spaying and shots — another 300 bucks.

I read on the internet how important it is to start housebreaking immediately and to count on it taking a week. So damn it, I took a week off from work. And every time Kisser got up from his nap, I carried her outside to the pee place and waited… and waited. Finally, success, followed instantly by a treat and massive praise. But despite my diligence, Kisser had a few accidents, including one vomit. But yes, after a week, she was trained.

But Kisser would not sleep in her crate. The first night, I put her in and within seconds, she was whimpering, the sweetest damn whimper you ever heard. I needed to sleep so I moved the crate from the kitchen to my bedroom. She still whimpered, and whimpered. At some God-forsaken hour, I got up, put a towel on the far corner of the bed — I was NOT going to have pee or poop on my blanket — and I lowered her onto the towel. Immediately, she stopped whimpering, curled up, and went to sleep —She was doing a great job of training me. The only thing, by the time I got up in the morning, Kisser was no longer at the foot of the bed. She was curled up around my warmest spot — my crotch. And when I started to get up, she jumped on me, licked my face, we went out, and she did her business like a pro.

After a week, I was grateful I had Kisser. I could see why they call a dog man's best friend. So you can imagine how I felt when after eight days, the doorbell rang. It was a neighbor. She said, "I had just gotten a puppy when, in the middle of the night, I got a call from a hospital 200 miles away — My dad had had a heart attack. I was frantic. I was so frantic, I forget to leave you a note and I forgot all about the dog. My dad died, we had the funeral, and when I came back and saw the crate, I remembered. I am so sorry, so so sorry. Thank you so much for taking care of my puppy. Can I have her back now?"

Rock Star

The author and Hachi again. Own work.

My dog, Rock Star (Rocky for short) is the world's sweetest dog. I wanted to share him with more than just passersby. It merely required me to be a little outrageous.

For example, I passed the local elementary school at recess. Rocker and I walked on campus, I let him off the leash, whereupon he bounced up to group after group, tail wagging, and nuzzling up for a pet or hug.

Then, for fun, kids started to run away, and Rocky raced after. Never have you heard such yelps of delight. When the supervisor stomped over, I fake-apologized profusely and we left, my tail between my legs, but not really.

Then there were the shut-ins. For example, on my walks, I occasionally saw old people staring out their window. I came to the door and explained that Rocky would love to say hi. Between my big smile and Rocky's wagging his entire rear half, even most scared, senile people gave it a shot — and never regretted it. Before I've left, they're usually back in their chair with Rocky on their lap cuddling.

Then there were the nursing homes. I never asked permission before coming in — I was afraid they'd say crap like "Insurance regulations don't allow pets." I just strutted in like I owned the place and if someone tried to stop me, I just announced, "Service dog" and strode on. It usually worked. I then followed the signs to the TV room, activities room, wherever I sense there'd' be a covey of residents. There, the comatose denizens' heads usually rose from somnolence. Some even levitated from their wheelchairs and became more alert than if I had given them an upper.

I did that for years and finally, my Rocky died. I invited everyone we had visited to the funeral, which was held in a pet cemetery. Four hundred people (and more than a few dogs) showed up and many gave touching eulogies, but none like Mildred Epps'. An attendant wheeled her hospital bed — yes, a hospital bed —up to the grave site and Mildred wheezed, "At every funeral, people crow about how great the person was, even if it was a crack-dealing car-jacker. But no praise is more deserved than what we're saying about Rocky. May we humans, supposedly superior creatures, live up to who Rock Star was." The applause was greater and, indeed, more deserved, than for human rock stars.

Best in Class

Eddy Van 3000, Flickr, CC 2.0

I was bored with teaching — Most kids cared less about learning than about the 3 f's: friends, fooling around, and flirting, even though they're just 5th graders.

And then there's the mounting paperwork — reporting mandates for the district, county, state, and feds. That leaves no time to give and therefore correct writing assignments, which would do a lot more good than all that bureaucratic crap.

And then there's the curriculum. School has always been boring but the Common Core Curriculum, in the name of high standards (as defined by ivory-tower academics), has increased boredom to a whole new level. Here is just one of its many standards, quoted verbatim: #5.G.A. http://tinyurl.com/ycyrprm3

Use a pair of perpendicular number lines, called axes, to define a coordinate system, with the intersection of the lines (the origin) arranged to coincide with the 0 on each line and a given point in the plane located by using an ordered pair of numbers, called its coordinates. Understand that the first number indicates how far to travel from the origin in the direction of one axis, and the second number indicates how far to travel in the direction of the second axis, with the convention that the names of the two axes and the coordinates correspond (e.g., x-axis and x-coordinate, y-axis and y-coordinate).

Who the hell, other than maybe engineers, architects, and supervising carpenters, needs to know that? Yet every student, every student, is required to be taught that — I doubt that many *learn* it, let alone the myriad other "Standards." Even now in adulthood, I've never used such Standards. Have you?

So I had an idea. What if our class rescued a dog from the pound that was about to be "euthanized" and adopted it? Each night, one child would take the dog home, care for it, and bring it back in the morning. What a meaningful and fun way to teach responsibility! And we'd save a life.

I asked the principal but she said no: "Fleas, allergies, and our insurance wouldn't cover it." I gave perfectly reasonable answers: There are now excellent flea meds that need be used only monthly, which of course we'd use. We'd get a hypoallergenic dog, like a poodle mix. Regarding insurance, we'd speak with the carrier — I'm sure that for a nominal amount, we could add a rider." She still said no.

I appealed to the school board. No.

I then tried asking our school's foundation's biggest donor if she'd plead our case. She did and we got permission to do a trial month. If there was a problem, we agreed that the dog would be returned to the pound.

So we signed up for alerts at the local dog-rescue sites, saying we need a dog that is hypoallergenic, gentle and kind, and at risk of being "euthanized."

Two weeks later, we got a notice that a candidate was available. While sweet and hypoallergenic, she'd soon be killed because she was ten years old and, in candor, had an ugly face.

When we got to her cage in the pound, despite the face, it was unanimous love at first sight. The dog sidled against our legs and, if we bent down, kissed us. We asked the attendant the dog's name and she said the dog was a stray with no tags so we could name it whatever we want. The kids wanted to name it after Taylor Swift, so we quickly agreed on Swifty.

And all went well. The first night's caretaker was a shy girl who came alive with Swifty. The second night, it was a boy who's a bit of a bully but was sweet with Swifty—We knew he treated Swifty well that night because in the morning, Swifty stayed by his side.

Alas, the third night was a nightmare. The child, Jessica, was a particularity caring one and when she got home, she felt that Swifty's collar was a bit tight, so she loosened it just a bit, and it seemed to her that it wouldn't come off. But when Jessica took Swifty for a walk, the dog pulled, slipped out of the collar, and ran away. Jessica ran after her but soon lost sight of her. Jessica ran back to her apartment, she and her parents drove around, yelling for Swifty while the mom called the teacher, the cops, and the pound. Of course, even though the school was a half mile away, probably too far for Swifty to find, especially because she had only been there for three days, they drove to the school and Jessica stayed by the classroom door while her parents ran around yelling "Swifty." At 10 PM, exhausted, they gave up.

But in the morning, there was Swifty, sleeping in front of the classroom door. I guess after some hours of exploration, it was sleep time and she knew where her bread was buttered or, I should say, where her kibble was served.

I'll bet there has been more learning of value, more caring, more responsibility in these first few days with Swifty than anything I have ever taught — even "Use a pair of perpendicular number lines…"

No Soap

Courtesy: Daysofourlivesspoilers

A few months ago, my husband and I had escaped from the big city to a cottage 15 miles northeast of Grants Pass, Oregon.

I say "I" because Jerry, my dear husband of 51 years died suddenly two months ago.

Now it's just me, or I should say, me, my little doggie Angel, and my soap operas, especially Days of Our Lives, which I've been watching since I was 15.

Angel sits on my lap and we laugh and we cry. My best "friends" are the Days of Our Lives characters, especially dear Maggie and her late husband Mickey. Maggie has been on the show since 1973 and Mickey died in 2010. I'm still grieving…and yes, watching the reruns. I stream.

I talk to the TV, urging the characters, consoling the characters, and, okay, I also talk to my doggie. For example, "Angel, I hate to admit it but I like you better than most people. I can always count on your kindness and your cuddles. And all I need to do is give you kibble. Out here in the wilderness, I don't even need to walk you — You just go out the doggie door. And I know you love me, so you won't run away. You'll always come back, just like my dear, dear Jerry."

It was an unusually windy rainstorm, so I was especially grateful to be in my usual soft chair with Angel on my lap. We were watching Days of Our Lives' 50th-anniversary show for the third time — Maggie had become crippled and Mickey gave her red shoes hoping that someday, they'd dance again.

And then the power went out. With the howling wind and sheets of rain, Angel and I needed to stay inside and hoped the power would come back quickly. But out in the boonies, I knew it was an unlikely hope.

After a day cooped up and with no TV, you can imagine how I felt when someone knocked on my door. Who could have come out in this weather? When I opened the door, it was my neighbor's 12-year-old son. "Come in! Please!"

I would have thought he'd race in but, shoulders hunched, he just shuffled in without a word.

"I've rarely seen you. Why would you come out in this mess?"

"My parents made me. They said you were old and I should check on you."

"I am old but I'm okay except it's not fun having no electricity. Can I get you some cookies?" He nodded.

"Do you want to tell me a little about you?"

"I dunno. I'm 12. My name is Harris."

I thought but didn't say, "Oh my God, Harris is the name of an evil character on Days of Our Lives — a kidnapper and attempted murderer." But I just said, "Harris, that's a nice name."

Just then, the lights came back on. Angel danced around — She was happier than I was. Harris said, "Well, I guess I should go now."

"Want to watch a little TV with me?"

"Uh, we don't have TV, so okay."

"Would you mind if we watch Days of Our Lives. I stream it so I can watch whatever episode whenever I want."

He shrugged.

I know all the episodes, so I chose one in which a pre-teen boy is the main character. Because Harris was distant, I picked the episode in which the Theo is diagnosed with autism.

Harris stared and then got teary. I asked if he wanted to talk about it. He shook his head and said, "I should go now."

I said, "You can come back…if you'll watch another episode."

For the first time, he smiled and left, walking just a bit straighter.

I lifted Angel onto my lap and after I finish writing this, we'll watch another episode.

The Prince and Princess of Duke City

Courtesy, SeventyFourImages

I'm a landscape architect who works for the Duke City government. My current project is Safer Duke. Our parks have lots of crime and I'm replacing high shrubs with low ones so miscreants can't hide. Also, each park will have an artificial babbling brook — We hope that gentle waters will make arguments less likely to escalate. For the park that abuts a high-crime housing project, I'm designing a high thorny vine — a natural barbed-wire fence.

I work remotely, which is great, so every hour or two, I can get out of my chair and take my dog Princess for a walk, for example, our lunchtime walk to our favorite cafe.

Once, as we were crossing the street to the cafe, two motorcyclists wearing Duke Overlords black leather jackets were approaching. I was going to stop but one of them nodded at me, so Princess and I proceeded. But apparently the other motorcyclist wasn't looking and ran me over.

Princess escaped and ran to the cafe but I was crushed under the motorcycle, its hot muffler pressed against my leg. The motorcyclist tried to pull his bike up but couldn't and it fell again on my leg. The second time, he succeeded, jumped on his bike, and the two of them roared away.

The cafe owner raced out and called 911 while holding Princess. When the paramedics put me into the ambulance, I said, "Please let my dog come with me." One said, "It's against the rules but…"

Long story short, the burn was so deep that my leg had to be amputated and fitted with a prosthetic leg. Fortunately, the C-4 gets you a pretty natural gait, that is, after months of rehab and yes, pain.

Princess was my best rehab coach — After all, she had to go out to do her business. So, much as I usually would have preferred to stay in bed, we went out every couple hours, for her benefit and ultimately mine.

After months of this — and I really should spare you the details, we walked again for the first time to the café, albeit with a cane. The owner took a picture of us, and the next time I came, he had enlarged it and hung it on the wall with a caption: The Prince and Princess of Duke City.

Trying

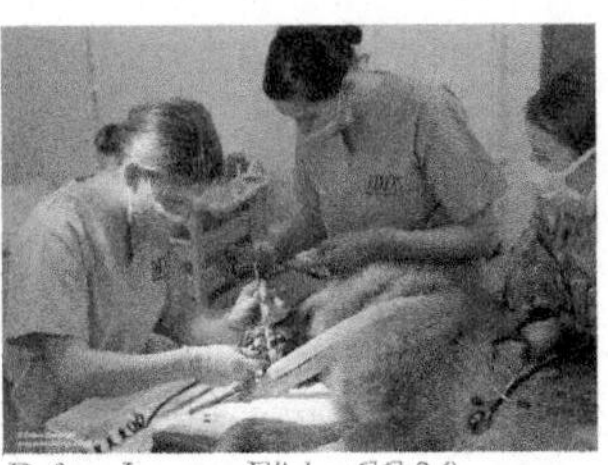
Defence Imagery, Flickr, CC 2.0

Even since a vet came to my high school biology class, I wanted to be a vet. but when I got to college, those hard science courses convinced me I wasn't smart enough. Fortunately, with taxpayer help, I figured I could make enough money as a vet-tech.

I got hired by a local vet and quickly got more and more responsibility. I started just by taking notes but soon got to draw blood and then to assist in surgery.

The vet did many successful surgeries but one time, a buffed, tattooed man brought in a dog that had been mauled in a dog fight. The doctor had to fix deep gashes, slipped and cut a nerve. When the dog woke, he couldn't walk well at all — He collapsed after just a few steps. The doctor was mad at herself and asked me whether I thought she should put the dog down and just tell the dog-fighter owner that the dog died unavoidably in surgery. I felt I should leave the decision to her, so I just said, "It's a personal decision. Do what you think is wise."

She decided to tell the owner that his dog would never walk again and the owner said, "No biggie. Put him down."

I couldn't live with that so I asked the vet if I could adopt the dog. She advised against it: "It would be too difficult, for you and for the dog." It *was* too hard — I couldn't get even get him to go out to "do his business."

I asked the doctor if I could be the one to put the dog down. She nodded and, my hand shaking, I gave the injection, and cried.

I think I'm going to try again to do pre-vet.

A Hypochondrial Undertaker

Courtesy: Cleveland.

Even as a child, I was scared of dying. When I was around 10, I recall lying in bed thinking that the average man lives to be 80, so I have about 87% left.

It only got worse from there. I was pre-med mainly to deal with any diseases I'd get, but that made me worse — I developed half the diseases I learned about. So I switched to Religious Studies but couldn't believe in a God who'd allow billions of people, including children, to die in agony of cancer.

Then I tried therapy. And no, my mother's overprotectiveness didn't cause my fear of dying. Nor was there some trauma, no matter how much the therapist tried to dredge one up. And the cognitive-behavioral shrink helped only a bit: "Distract yourself by doing something constructive." She also recommended desensitization, like stand in a hospital lobby and when you can do that, walk a ward, and so on. It didn't help enough. In desperation, I decided to try the ultimate desensitization: become an undertaker. But that made it worse — cleaning up those corpses for open caskets? OMG.

The one thing that really helped — very temporarily, you'll see why — was when a woman named Melanie came in wanting to pre-pay for her funeral. I was taken with her. Not only was it kind of Melanie to save her family the strain and cost, Melanie was about my age…and cute.

But the next day, I get a call that Melanie had died — suicide! She was a mess — Cleaning her up, Oh!

As I usually do, I went to supervise Melanie's interment and afterward, when I reached my hearse, a little dog looked up at me with sad eyes. I opened the door for myself, and the dog jumped in!

I found myself caring for Daisy like a person, no, better than a person — Daisy is like a baby who never grows up. And would you believe, focusing so much on her and loving her snuggling with me in my easy chair. in bed, sometimes even on my lap as I'm driving the hearse, I'm somehow less worried about dying. I'd be lying if said I'm cured but it's sure better than what I got from "trauma-informed therapy."

A Lucky Dog

Hachi again. own work.

I have been a lucky dog right from the beginning. You see, I was born in a field and my mommy took such good care of me — I got all the milk and all the warmth I wanted. I loved nuzzling with my brothers and sisters.

Another piece of good luck was when I was just striking out on my own (I was seven weeks old), and Don, Mary, and their son, Tom were driving by. They stopped, saw that I had no collar, let alone a chip, and gently put me in the car, right on Tom's lap. I knew this was going to be good. And yes, they turned out to be my forever family.

I have such memories. I had heard through the bonevine that many dogs have to sleep in crates or even outside in a doghouse. But from Night One, I slept in Tom's bed and he didn't even make me sleep at the foot of the bed. He let me nuzzle right in, just like I did with my mommy.

And we had a backyard, an enclosed backyard, so I could romp and do my business without my family worrying I'd run away. I must admit that if there were an opening, I'd be tempted to go out and explore, but fenced-in was fine.

I got plenty chance to explore when Don, Mary, or Tom took me on a walk — Oh the sights and smells — other people, flowers, other doggies! And oh when we took a trip somewhere — all new sights and smells. Of course, my favorite was Carmel — There's an off-leash beach. I loved going in the waves, well, up to my ankles. Further out would have been scary.

And most restaurants in Carmel have a patio so I didn't have to wait in the car. One restaurant even has a doggie menu! I always ordered their Quarter Hounder.

When I got older, my joints started to hurt. The vet said I have arthritis. And over the years, it got worse. It has gotten so bad that it really hurts to walk. And now, most of the time, I can't even make myself get up to pee.

So my family took me to the vet. I'm writing to you while on the vet's table. She just came in and gave me a shot. It's making me sleepy and Don, Mary, and Tom are all crying, I don't know why. I just know that I'm getting very sleepy, so I'll say goodbye for now.

The Dogs Yin and Yang

The dogs, Yin and Yang, natch, own a dog food store. Indeed, they are Yin and Yang.

Pixabay, CC

Yin doesn't even wait for a shelf to be empty before restocking it, even the 30-pound bags of dog food. Meanwhile, Yang sniffs around or just stares into space. Yin asks, no begs, Yang to help and he promises he will, "in a minute," that usually is three and sometimes is never.

If a customer comes in a bit after closing time, Yin will stop cleaning up and let the customer in — She doesn't mind working a bit later. Ying, at his best, sighs, and at his worst, guilt-trips her: "Don't we work enough?" Yin thought, "You barely work at all."

When there's a minute with no customers, Yin cleans: the powder from the dog food bags and, of course, when a doggie pees or poops. She jumps into action as though she's almost looking forward to it, although inside, she dislikes it. She just thinks, "It's part of the job." Yang doesn't jump and helps only when Yin gives him the, "I've had it with you" stare.

Finally, Yin had reached her breaking point: "Yang, if you don't start pulling your weight, I'm going to call Animal Control — You're just one big nuisance. And you know what happens there, especially to a cur like you."

That's what Yang needed. No, he'll never be as diligent as Yin, but images of him getting killed in the pound kept him out of the, well, doghouse.

A Dog Sitter

Hachi and me again. Photo credit: Courtesy, Dianne Woods

I'm having a hard time staying motivated as a barista. I have lasted longer than most — I'm 40. But is this all there is for me?

So when business is slow, I think. I think, what the hell can I do to have a life more meaningful than a decaf chai latte with oat milk?

I think I should do something for dogs. I can't have a dog in my apartment but I grew up with a dog, and it indeed was my best friend.

Then I came on an idea, not a good one probably, but here it is. I'm a shy person and have no money. So the best I can come up with is to sit at a dog park, sometimes at a train station, and hold up this sign:

Adopt a rescue; save a life.

Spay/neuter your doggie — dog pounds will kill fewer.

No dog fights. You're better than that.

I sit with my sign every day after work. I'm not ready to give up — People may need to see the sign many times before it changes their behavior. After all, everyone is trying to persuade everyone of so many things.

So I wait and I wait, and although I doubt I'm making much of a difference, I do feel better about being a barista.

Top Dog

Martin Varel, LibreShot, Public Domain

Like human political campaigns, the one for Top Dog was a dog fight. For example, in the last debate, Pit Bull Pete actually took a hunk out of Penny Poodle.

And as in human campaigns, slogans are rife: A Bone in Every Bowl, More Belly Rubs for Bow-Wows, A Dog's Place is in the Bed, Doggies in Diners and, stealing from dog trainer, Barbara Woodhouse, "There are no bad dogs; only bad owners." (Privately, Pete knows that's BS but it gets votes, from liberals and especially from bad dogs. Pete shrugs, "A vote is a vote."

Using DogPark, the canine social-media app, Pete's PR director staged *Pee-In at the Pound.* 150 dogs showed up and left an olfactory message. And the media covered it — Talk about yellow journalism.

Pete has amassed a pack of activist volunteers, which he calls The Wolf Pack. They go house to house and if no one answers or the human doesn't seem supportive, on the doormat, they leave a brown message. Their motto: "We don't take no shit."

Of course, Pete knows to play good-cop, bad cop, so he fronts his wife, a Shitzu to say what a family-dog Pit-Bull Pete is while smilingly holding up her litter of Bull-Shitzu puppies.

Not surprisingly, Pete won in what Penny Poodle called a mudslide. Penny is trying yet again for canine campaign reform but PupPolling puts the odds of success at 100 to 1.

A Dog's Search for His Father

pxhere, CC

I lived with my mother until she died at age 13, around 90 in human years.

Now I'm alone, 11 and a male, so I probably won't live that long. I never knew my father and hadn't really cared to. As far as I knew, he was just some German Shepherd mix that my mom hung out with in The Vale.

But now, aware of my mortality and, okay, feeling lonely, I decided to try to find my father. I figured I'd start with the only obvious place: where I was born, The Vale.

There, I met an owl. I described what my dad probably looks like — My mom had told me. And the owl said, "I think I know who you're talking about — There's a crotchety, very old dog who lives in the cave over there."

I peered inside and was met with a weak growl— The dog looked like I'd imagined he would, but older. He crept out, teeth bared. He wheezed, "What do you want?"

I asked, "Did you hang out with a shepherd mix many years ago?"

"I did. We felt good roaming together and we slept in this cave."

"I can't be sure but I think I'm your son."

Quieter, tireder, now that he wasn't on alert, he whispered, "I think I can see myself in you." And he lay down.

I toddled over, rested my feet on his belly, and he sighed.

"Dogs are Just Dirty Scavengers"

"Dogs are just dirty scavengers," Professor Harden said to his zoology class.

Defense Visual Information Distribution Service, Public Domain

"People's love of dogs speaks to thirst for connection but that's a false one. Dog nuzzling, kissing — filthy animals, they lick feces —so-called 'loyalty' is just self-preservation. Love? Hah!"

What then occurred is ironic. You see, a couple years later, Harden was driving home, mulling his class's various "losers," when a small dog raced into the street and Dr. Harden's car hit him. To his credit, Harden didn't hit and run; he stopped. The dog was motionless except for quivering. Harden picked her up and took her to a vet who said, "That dog was lucky. She'll be scared for a few days but will be okay."

The dog had no tags and no chip, and the vet said, "So, what do you want to do with her?" Harden's guilt and the dog's dark eyes worked on him: "I'll keep her for those few days."

Schooled in the science of dog training, Harden got an economy crate and cheap kibble, threw an old towel in and pushed the dog inside. "Bedtime — Yowling or not, that dog, who I will not name, will sleep in the crate. I'll put it in the basement so it doesn't keep me up."

In the morning, Harden came down to feed and walk the dog. The dog's tail wagged wildly and pawed the crate. Harden opened it and she, yes, nuzzled against him. "Animal instinct," he scoffed. He threw a handful of kibble in the bowl and took her out: "Do your business."

Long story short, "a few days" kept getting extended and before long, Harden told his class the story of the now-named, "Snookums" and said, "Everything I said about dogs is true but just maybe there's a *little* room in the equation for that love thing."

A Doggie Hits a Club on New Year's Eve

My owner loves me, so he took me with him to the "New Year's Eve Bash" at the Cool Club.

Hachi. Own work

$200 a person for hats, horns, a glass of cheap champagne, and mini hot dogs (love the name)? That's a lot of kibble even though I got in free despite my owner thinking of me as a family member.

Ouch, the music! So loud, no one can talk. And we dogs, who have sensitive hearing — Is it time to go yet?

At midnight, all the guys in their penguin suits and the women in their glittery nonsense stared at some ball drop — covered with rhinestone (or is it "man-made diamond" — Love those marketers) like it was the vote-count in a tight presidential election.

And then, they kissed — Some looked like they were doing it out of obligation. Then, most of the obligation ones tiptoed out. Others danced, with most women looking like they were having an orgasm, the men a root canal.

Finally, we left. I would have rather he had left me home. I think *he'd* rather have stayed home. The food would have been better, the music nicer, and I'm better company than the people at the can't-talk Cool Club.

Hats-and-horns-hoo-hah at $200 a pop. Dogs are smarter than people.

A Doggie's New Year's Resolutions

I know, I know, resolutions are a waste — We all break them, but they provide hope for a better tomorrow. Maybe if I tell you my resolutions, I might keep them past January 1.

Hachi, own work

I really should eat more slowly — I'll enjoy it for longer. Unfortunately, I've told myself this for years and by supper on January 1, I'm back to inhaling my kibble.

I want to be less persistent in begging. Yes, occasionally my persistence pays in an extra VeggieDent, but usually not. Besides, it annoys Bob — He's my owner. I love Bob and don't want him annoyed.

Bob prefers me at the *foot* of the bed but, especially in winter, it feels soooh much comfier to press against his side. If I find myself up in the middle of the night, I think I'll sidle over.

In the morning, I don't like to wait so long for him to walk me. So as soon as I get up and see Bob starting to stir — I don't want to wake him from a *sound* sleep — I'll lick his face.

Bob gets frustrated when I take too long to find just the right spot to pee. I should try to pee faster.

At work, I'm going to try to nuzzle at his feet more. Yes, I'm curious about everything going on around me in the office, but Bob loves when I'm at his feet, and I like it too, including the smell of his feet.

But when Bob has to travel, I am going to put my paw down about going to the kennel — I will refuse to get out of the car. I will have a dogsitter stay with me at my house — Period!

Service Dog

Ebtimes, CC

I'm a lawyer, so I care that laws be followed. So when I saw someone bring a little mutt into the supermarket, I scoffed, "Dog in supermarket?!"

She said, "Service dog."

I smirked, "Right."

She: "Want to see his tag?"

Me: You can buy those on the internet.

She: I'll bet most people think you're a jerk.

Me: Don't change the subject.

She: That's the real subject.

Me: I'm happy with my life.

She: Even though most people think you're a jerk?

Me: (I wasn't sure it's true but I said), "Most people think I'm a good guy. But that's not the question. The question is, why are you bringing a non-service dog into the supermarket?"

She: You *are* avoiding the real question. And you can't be happy if you're obese, eating yourself into an early grave.

Me: What gives you the right?!

She: You started it. You aren't worth engaging with. I'm done.

Me: Good.

I feigned indifference but as I walked away, my face twitched and I couldn't stop it.

I peeked to see if she noticed. She was looking right at me, and she smiled knowingly.

I tried to forget it. I can't. Am I a jerk? Am I eating myself into an early grave?

The Sniff

Kingofthedead, Wikimedia. CC0

Sure, I first check out if the dog's teeth are bared but if it passes that screen, I go right for the genitals — I don't know why humans don't.

Usually, the smell is just okay, but today, OMG: olfactory nirvana! And then I looked at her. Wow: A poodly mix. And she seemed to like me — She went right for *my* holy spot, then wagged her tail and squealed with delight!

My owner — actually I prefer "caretaker" — trained me to not pull but I couldn't resist. I needed to get close to her — You know, love at first sight. Fortunately, my caretaker recognized when rules should be broken, and soon the doggie and I were nuzzling.

My caretaker laughed and her caretaker laughed and said magic words, "These two should have a playdate!"

This is going to be the best Valentine's Day ever.

A Judgmental Dog

Hachi and me again. Own work

A mean person adopted me for Christmas and today, New Year's Eve, dumped me on College Ave.

I didn't want to be a stray. I didn't even want to be alone on New Year's Eve. I had to find myself a new owner *today*.

I didn't want another — forgive the canine expression, bitch — so I kept my soulful eyes and floppy ears out for my forever owner, actually I prefer "caretaker."

Alas, most people just walked by flat-faced, with no more than a passing glance that said that they're too busy to look at a dog for more than a second. I guess people in Berkeley are busy with things more important to them than a stray dog. Or maybe they're just self-absorbed.

Finally, a guy stopped but just petted my head and strode on.

Then another guy — and this guy worried me — Somehow, his face looked mean, and he crept up to me but not in a nice way — and I was right. He shoved me. I wasn't hurt but my feelings were hurt. Are all people bad? I can understand why some people say they like dogs better than people.

It had started to rain, so I thought I'd have to give up and shelter in some doorway for New Year's Eve and probably into the New Year.

But then, it was like out of a fairy tale. A half-block away, I saw this man, woman, and a girl. The girl spotted me. We dogs have good hearing, so I heard her cry out, "Look at that doggie. I want a doggie. I want a doggie!" The man and woman looked at each other, and she pulled them to me. I liked *this*!

So I wagged my tail as wildly as I could, without trying my body swayed with excitement, and as they approached, I sidled up, and rested my head on the girl's legs.

The girl said, "I want him. I want him!" The man and women looked at each other and then at the girl, and the woman said, "A dog is a big responsibility. It's like a baby who never grows up. Will you promise to feed him?" "Yes." "Will you walk him, even in the rain?" "I promise!"

The man picked me up and nestled me in her arms, they walked on, and then gently put me in their car.

And so I think I have not only a place to go for New Year's Eve but my forever home. I am soooh happy. I will be a good doggie, I promise.

A Worry-Wart Hound

Annie Thorne, Flickr, CC 2.0

Hi, I'm Chiller. My owner sure misnamed me — I'm a worry-wart. I don't just yowl like other hounds do, my whole body quivers at the littlest thing: a gust of wind, a dog that's even a little bigger than I am, and don't even mention lightning.

I'm especially careful when we're crossing the street. I don't mean to say that my owner isn't careful, it's just that I'm neurotic — I look both ways *twice*.

But sometimes, no matter how careful you are, shit is unavoidable. We had done our usual preparation to cross the street when a thumping car squealed around the corner and smashed into me. Thank God, my owner was okay. The car sped off and I was lying there in 10 pain. I'd never yelped so loudly. I didn't think my owner could pick me up — I weigh 50 pounds — but the adrenaline gave him the strength. He groaned all the way back home, lowered me into the car, and drove me to my vet.

I am talking to you on my vet's table. She gave me a shot and the pain went away but I don't think she can fix me. My vet usually was so calm but now, she is working very quickly on my leg and on the rest of my body. Hey, I'm fading. Hmm, I wish I had been less of a worry-wart: It spoiled the good times and although I knew that, I just couldn't stop — I guess we have to accept ourselves. Hey, I'm getting very sleepy, very, very sleepy, so I'm going to say good-bye.

A 12-Year-Old Talks to Her Doggie

Pexels, CC0

Hi, my name is Lily and I'm 12. There are things I feel I can't talk about even with my best friend. So I talk to my doggie, Mei-Mei. Here's what I said to her today. It's not word-for-word but you'll get the idea:

Who am I, really? Yes, I'm biracial and that's cool but what else? I'm smart but there are smarter girls. I'm pretty I guess — At least my parents say so. But there are prettier girls, like Jasmine.

And I got my period, but am I straight? Gay? Bisexual? It's cool to be trans. Would I be that? I don't think so. But when will I develop breasts, real breasts? Will I always be chocolate chips? I guess that would be okay.

I still don't like boys much. Should I worry about that? No. A lot of boys are immature; some still even pull girls' hair. And my schoolbooks, and TV, and movies tell us that most boys and men are worse than girls and women, I mean like — what pops into my mind — the movies Frozen, Moana, Mulan, Matilda, Princess and the Frog — The girls are always better than the boys and especially the men. I wonder what boys seeing all that must feel like.

I worry more about my privilege. School tells me I'm privileged and have to give it up. But my parents worked hard to earn what they're calling privilege. But I'd be afraid to say that in class.

Oh well, I'm soooh, soooh grateful to have you, Mei-Mei! Want to go for a walk?

A College Student Talks to His Dog

NegativeSpace, CC

I couldn't tell my parents. I couldn't even tell my friends — I think college has been a bad use of my time and my parents' money. But I wanted to talk it out, so I decided to talk to my dog, Charlie.

Charlie, I don't have the guts to quit — I mean, it's hard enough to get a good job *with* a college degree. But God, I have a hard time even motivating myself to go to class, let alone study hard for tests. The stuff feels unimportant or like brainwashing. My best friends are Cliff's

Notes and SparkNotes. I haven't yet descended to buying term papers on the Net, in part because some professors use software to check for that. But I'm increasingly tempted.

The social life is fine but $300,000 for four years of play time? Feels like a very expensive four-year summer camp.

I mean, if I were smart enough to be pre-med or could likely become a good lawyer or something, okay. But I'm your typical psych major — 3.0 GPA and I haven't impressed any professor enough to expect to get more than a blah recommendation.

But what would I do if I didn't finish college? Of course, first I'd have to escape from my father yelling at me, but after that? The military? I'm not the type and besides, I don't want to risk having my head blown off. An apprenticeship? Maybe but it's four years long and not easy to get. Besides, do I want to become an electrician or a plumber? Not really. Self-employment sounds good but it's scary. I'm not Mr. Risk Taker.

So Charlie, what the hell should I do? Okay, okay, I know you won't answer me but I love you anyway. Okay, here's a treat.

An Israeli Veteran Talks to Her Dog

Thru the Glass, Flickr, CC 2.0

Hello, my name is Dahlia. I just finished my required service in the Israeli army. Part of me is honored to defend our tiny state of Israel. But yes, I have mixed feelings now.

Even though our country is much more open to debate than is Gaza or any of the large Muslim countries that surround us, I'm shy by nature, so I feel most comfortable talking about it to my sweet dog, Luna.

Today, I decided to talk to her not in sentences but to just free-associate whatever word or phrase came to mind. Here's what I recall:

Palestinian kids--So sad. Israeli overreaction. World will hate us more than ever. Forever? Antisemitism. The Israeli people. The Jewish people. Scientists, filmmakers, women's rights, minority rights — Arabs serve in the Knesset. Arabs are 20% in Israel, Jews in Muslim countries: Zero. Will Israel be destroyed? Hamas. Hamas schools — train kids to kill all Jews. From the river to the sea. Jihad, rockets, my sister — fuck the terrorists — music festival, kibbutz, cafes, buses, bar-mitzvahs, bat-mitzvahs, tunnels, tunnels, tunnels. We gave Hamas Gaza 20 years ago — We're not "occupiers." Hezbollah, Islamic Jihad, Al-Aqsa Martyr Brigade, PLO, Iran, regional war, nuclear, nuclear war. Nuclear war — Oh my God!

Dear Luna, I sometimes don't like Israel but I love Israel and I love you sweet, sweet Luna. Come here — Let me give you a hug.

A Cheese Clerk Talks to His Dog

FreeStock, CC

I have a bachelor's degree, so I feel embarrassed to tell people that I'm perfectly happy being a clerk at the cheese counter in a supermarket.

But I like to process things and not just cheese. So today, I talked with my dog, Cheddar, about why I like it, why I'm not ambitious like everyone else.

Dear Cheddar, many of my friends don't like their job. Usually, they say they're putting up with crap because they feel they have to pay dues before getting a good job. But I know a lot of older people with a "good" job who are overworked, underpaid, stressed, or feel they're making little difference.

It's not just that my job is chill. It's not just that the hours are regular — No one's going to call me at home to say they need a brie, now! I satisfy nearly every customer

— We sell good cheeses at a fair price. And I get to give out free samples. Everyone loves a freebie and I like giving them.

The pay's not great but with a roommate, I can make it.

The only thing I gotta watch out for is eating too much cheese. A little is fine but…

So, dear Cheddar, do you think I'm fooling myself and sooner than later, I'll want a "real" career but won't be hireable because who'd want to hire a cheese clerk?

I dunno but, in the meantime, Cheddar, how about a belly rub?

A Beauty Queen Talks to Her Dog

Quinn Dombrowski, Flickr, CC 2.0

I'm feeling insecure and, you'll laugh, but I feel most comfortable talking about it to my dog, Lucy. Here's kinda what I just said to her.

From when I was a little girl, they always called me pretty, but never smart. And it's true, I'm not. I always have been a little slower to pick things up than most people are. I'm not even sure I have a lot of common sense. Behind my back, I hear that people call me an airhead, space cadet, you know.

I've always done okay just using my looks — Guys, jobs, I won State Fair Beauty Queen back in 2012! But now, I'm 30 and I see my looks starting to fade and I'm getting scared.

To be honest, here in California where the job market is so hard, I can't see myself making good money, year after year. They make us feel guilty for wanting a wallet-husband — They still use the word, "Gold digger" — but if I'm honest, while I respect all those woman doctors, woman lawyers, woman executives, that's just not me. I think I really would (gulp) like to be a traditional housewife: keep house, have kids, and yes, be supported by my husband."

But how to find him? No more nightclubs — That's what got me in trouble with my first husband — He'd rather drink than talk. That says it all. But I do bad in classes, so that won't work for me. The gym? Maybe, but the people seem so judgmental — and I'm starting to get a belly and even a little cottage-cheese thighs. Set-ups? Yeah, I probably need to ask my friends, again. But this time I gotta tell 'em, no more bad boys, no matter how cute. Yes, decent-looking but he's gotta be stable and someone I can count on to bring home the bacon. He doesn't have to be rich, just middle class. That's not asking too much, right? I'm nice and I think I'd be a good homemaker and mommy. That's a fair deal, right?

Oh, sweet Lucy, oh, I forgot to feed you. I am so sorry. I'll do it right now. I love you, Lucy.

A Dancer Talks to Her Dog

I do ballet, and we all have to act like dance is everything. No one would dare express doubts. I'm not going to stick my neck out.

Courtesy, The Baxter

So today, I decided to spill my guts to my dog, Arabesque. Here's the essence of what I said.

I've put in all this time to learn ballet and, when I'm on stage, it's fun but it's getting to be less fun. And I'm on stage only a few minutes for every ten hours I'm rehearsing or practicing on my own.

And my feet are starting to get bad — No surprise. That's happening to all of us.

So Arabesque, I'm just about ready to quit. But to what? Teach dance? I'd still have to live with my parents. Something outside of dance? I have no idea what. I'm not going to be a computer programmer or a carpenter or a salesperson.

Arabesque, did I make a mistake putting all this time and effort into ballet? I can't think about it now. Arabesque, do you want to go for a walk, or watch me practice for my next performance?

A Musician Talks to His Dog

The author. Courtesy, Dianne Woods

Part of why I became a musician is because I'm an introvert, not social. I'm more comfortable playing. So when I want to talk, especially about something important, I talk, would you believe, to my dog, Billy. Here's a paraphrase of what I just said to him:

Yeah, I like being a musician but even though I'm a busy professional, I'm barely scraping by. Only the famous make real money. Is it time for me to grow up and get a straight job? Nah, I'm not ready for that yet.

I need to work on something:

My playing? I guess, but I'm pretty good.

My image? I probably need to be edgier — maybe a purple streak in my hair, maybe gyrate more at the keyboard, I dunno.

I probably should market myself more. Like send bigger bands some links to my SoundCloud and YouTubes. I've told myself to do that a lot of times, but I really should. I think this time, I will.

Hey, Billy, what do you think? Yeah, I know what you think. You think I should give you a treat. I already gave you two today but what the heck.

A CEO Talks to His Dog

madabandon, Flickr, CC 2.0

I still am the CEO but had to go on leave because my hip is so bad. Ironically, our nonprofit aims to increase the poor's access to health care. But it's biting me in the back or I should say, the hip. I've searched doctor after doctor and the best I can get is a four-month wait and, to be honest, I'm not sure how good a hip surgeon he is.

Even though I'm the CEO, I can't say a word about DEI— I'll likely get the 3 C's: Censure, Censor, and Cancel. The only "person" I can speak honestly to is my dog. Here is a paraphrase of what I said to her today:

Even though I've paid so much into the system when those we lobby for haven't, their activists, liberal politicians, medical schools, and nonprofits like ours, are clamoring for redistributing yet more to them.

And here I sit in such pain that I've had to take a leave of absence. I'm 55 and know that these are likely my last highly productive years. I want to be as contributory as I can, and the system increasingly won't let me.

Activists' pitches for yet more health-care redistribution are just the tip of the iceberg. I already pay more than half my income in taxes. The top 1% of earners pay 42.3% of the federal income tax. http://tinyurl.com/5fu2dxk7 Atop that, I pay much more when we include sales tax, property tax, car registrations, tolls, etc. I don't keep a dime until August, maybe September. The president of the United Autoworkers Union recently spawned a movement: "Eat the Rich!" http://tinyurl.com/2hnyrmj2 Most rich people work long and hard, delaying gratification, yes for money but also for contribution. Is that a fair way to treat such contributory citizens?

And I do have deep concern about illegal immigration, disproportionately people who haven't done well in their home country. And it doesn't bode well for their future law-abidingness that they chose to break our laws by coming here illegally and then take money from taxpayers, not just in health care but in, for example, education, welfare, and, of course, the cost of crime: Each victim of a mere smash-and-grab, let alone an assault, let alone rape or murder, is a human being who suffers unnecessarily.

Disproportionately, those crimes are committed by the poor. We've already spent $22 trillion on the poor for 50 years trying to close the achievement gap, http://tinyurl.com/ya8xxmxa yet the gap remains as wide as ever. http://tinyurl.com/3rwdkx27 Even the vaunted Head Start has largely failed. http://tinyurl.com/msu86uww Can we be optimistic that an answer lies in DEI as claimed by the likes of dozens-of-times accused plagiarist http://tinyurl.com/yey6m3fe and resigned Harvard president Claudine Gay? DEI's under-the-surface principle is to redistribute yet more from society's contributors to those less-so, heavily based on race. Does that provide a realistic basis for optimism for America's ascendancy, or for its decline?

Yet the Democrats, with the media's amplifying support, are doing what they can — while not damaging their re-election chances — to allow the illegality—The number of illegals entered since Biden took office is the most in history, more than two million, this year alone! http://tinyurl.com/4kphz7ee There are now 50 million foreign-born U.S. residents, also the highest in history. http://tinyurl.com/4sxpj2an The Democrats know that the illegals who will then become citizens as part of "comprehensive immigration reform" will overwhelmingly vote Democrat. What would Biden say to the millions of legal immigrants, of all backgrounds, who followed the law and entered legally?

I guess that every generation, when it gets old, thinks the younger generation is wrong-headed. I'm no exception.

Excuse me but my hip is killing me now. I need to take a pill and a nap.

Thank you, dear doggie. You're pretty much the only "person" to whom I can speak the truth. I love you.

A Salesman Turned Fundraiser Talks to His Dog

Antoni Shkraba, Pexels, CC

I shouldn't have chosen a career as a salesman and now, its nonprofit equivalent: fundraiser. I was seduced by the "infinite income potential," which turns out to be, at best, an overstatement. Too often, if you do too well, they cap your income, lower your commission rate, change your territory, some shit like that. Worse, selling, including nonprofit fundraising, is very stressful — Make your number or you get a worse prospect list, or even worse, you're out.

So when day is done, I need to process it all, and my favorite listener is my dog, Gretchen. Here's a paraphrase of what I said to her today. Admittedly it was a particularly bad day.

Gretchen, I thought I'd be happier pitching the museum than Dodge cars.

But it's as, well, dodgy. I can't help but worry about asking people to donate to an art museum. Yes, they're rich and yes, some of them got their money by stretching the truth, but so do I. And most of those people work hard for their money. Can I really look them in the eye and say that donating to an art museum or to a university that has plenty of money and too often Wokeizes its students are the best uses of their charity dollars when deep down I believe that, for example, cancer, Salvation Army, and Big Brothers and Sisters are better causes? I tried to get a job selling for a better cause than the art museum but competition for those is crazy.

Maybe it's time to cut my losses and throw a party for all the people who like me and ask them if they know of someone who could hire me for something different — I have no idea what that would be.

In the meantime, I'm going to take you for a walk, dear Gretchen. You can pee and I can de-stress.

An 85-Year-Old Talks to His Dog

Pexels, CC0

I hate that now I feel compelled to think mainly about my health or, more accurately, my lack of health.

I don't want to burden others with it, so I talk to my dog. Here's a paraphrase of what I just said to Daisy.

I probably just have a cold but I'm going to take a COVID test now. With all my comorbidities and old age's path downward to misery and death, maybe I should hope I get COVID and die of it. They say that respiratory diseases like pneumonia are among the easier ways to go — an old man's best friend

Old ***Man's*** best friend — Hmmph. Why, when we men have the ultimate deficit, we die six years younger http://tinyurl.com/5n6j4539 and live our last decade in worse health, no one gives a shit. All we see is another run for breast cancer. Yet if women are underrepresented in some field, there's massive redress. Hmmph. But I can't do anything about that; no one can. It's the Woke DEI unfairness. It's unstoppable because they've taken control of society's mind-molders: the schools, colleges, and media, even entertainment media.

I am scared of age's worsening pain. Yet I'm always reluctant to go to the doctor: They'll do tests that can confirm or even exceed my worst fears. And too often, they make mistakes. Oh I wish I could just suddenly not wake up, but not yet, I still enjoy life's little pleasures: coffee, conversation, and yes, you, sweet Daisy.

I sure would want my doctor to help me die if I were in bad pain, but the rules are so damn strict — You have to be compos mentis — Many people in bad pain aren't, and you must have less than six months to live. Why can't I off myself when I want — It's life's most personal decision and the government shouldn't invade that. They defend a woman's right to an abortion but not a person's decision on when life is too painful? Damn them.

I wonder what they'll say about me at my funeral. No doubt it will be BS that makes me look like a saint. The truth? I'd just a middling guy —In a world that goes from Old Milwaukee to Heineken, I'm a Bud.

Thank you, dear Daisy. I feel you're the only "person" I can say this stuff to.

Okay, now I'm going to take that COVID test and I'm not sure what to wish for.

Edgar and Goliath

Pixabay, CC

Edgar is disliked. His co-workers view him as rigid and too judgmental. His friends, even his relatives, keep their distance because he's argumentative and makes them feel less-than.

So an ever larger part of Edgar's relationships are with his dog. Now 65, Edgar mainly hangs out with his cockapoo, Goliath: He even talks to Goliath—to talk out problems, express frustrations with the world, speak words of love.

One night, Edgar said, "Goliath, I love you. I don't know how I'd cope if you died."

Edgar's daily rituals include Goliath. In the morning, Goliath wakes Edgar by kissing his face. Then, even when the Kansas winter is at its worst, Edgar gives Goliath a thorough walk. Edgar convinced his employer to allow Goliath to come to work. Edgar spends most of his lunch hour walking Goliath while eating a sandwich. After work, Edgar walks Goliath again, having trained him to carry the newspapers that were in front of people's houses to their front door. When watching TV at night, Goliath lay at Edgar's feet. And of course, Goliath sleeps in the bed with Edgar.

In the middle of one night, Edgar had a heart attack. Sensing something was wrong, Goliath tried to help in the only way he could—he licked Edgar's face, again and again. Alas, Edgar was too stricken to pick up the phone to dial 911. Suddenly, Edgar was still and Goliath returned to lie next to Edgar's leg.

In the morning, as usual, Goliath kissed Edgar's face but he didn't wake. Goliath started barking and barking. A neighbor heard it and, annoyed, called Edgar's phone number. No answer, so the neighbor, who had a key to the house, came in and saw the dead Edgar. The neighbor called the police, which took Edgar to the morgue and Goliath to the pound.

My Last Dog

Hachi and me., own work

It's so painful seeing your dog die. It was worst with my most recent sweetie, Donut. Maybe that was because my own death is next on the conveyor belt — I'm 85 and even after my knee replacement, I can't walk well, and being sedentary is bad. My walks have become shorter and less frequent — my age, my knees, and no further need to walk a dog. So I decided that Donut was my last doggie.

But I was lonely. It got to where my social life consisted mainly of saying hi to the Amazon delivery guy. So I thought, what could it hurt to *look*? So I went to the pound. Oh, the barking and yelping. It was easy to pass all the pit bulls and chihuahuas, the pound's predominant residents, but then there was this little poodly thing who, when I stopped to peek, leapt onto the front of the cage, whined, and wagged her tail.

When I looked more closely, I saw that she was missing a leg — I could understand why such a sweetie wouldn't be very adoptable. I could picture her getting "euthanized," and I just couldn't let it happen. Besides, with three legs, we'd be compatible — We'd both limp.

I thought about naming her Muffin, slightly healthier in name at least than Donut, but because of the three legs, I chose Trio. Indeed, we enjoyed our limpy walks — until I tripped on a raised sidewalk, reinjuring my knee. My limp had become a crawl and even three-legged Trio pulled me to go faster.

So I asked my 12-year-old neighbor, bookish Lenny, if he'd walk her once a day. Lenny would, twice, three times a day, knock on my door asking if Trio wanted a walk.

I realized I was selfish in keeping Trio. So I offered him to Lenny, and he and his parents happily agreed. I asked only for visitation rights. I'm kind of proud of myself. It seems like part of graceful aging.

Marty Nemko

TRUE STORIES OF MY DOGGIE, HACHI, AND ME

A Day in the Life of My Doggie

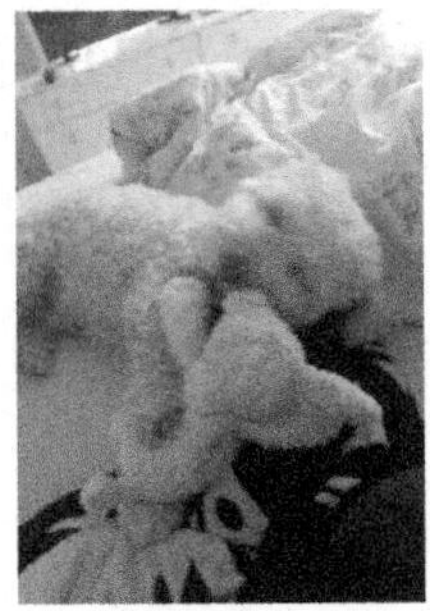

Hachi. Own work

I dote on my doggie. I thought I'd share a typical day. It just might make you a better dog owner — or should I say, caretaker. Or you might just laugh at me, someone who prides himself on being maximally productive, devoting so much time and energy to a mutt.

On waking, I'm careful not to wake my Hachi who, younger, needs more sleep. I dress quietly so not to wake him and then open the door to my home-office, which Hachi hears no matter how deeply he's sleeping. That's because it's the sound that food is nigh. He lifts his little head, I come over, say something like, "Good morning, sweet Hachi" and give him the first of the day's many belly rubs. He then jumps from the bed, tail wagging like he had never before seen food.

In my home-office, I put a handful of his $100-a-bag, top-rated Orijen dog food into a bowl and give him fresh water. Unlike with my previous dogs, for whom I could leave a self-dispensing food canister available when the mood strikes, that would make Hachi blimpoid. That, of course, is unhealthy for anyone, but my Hach (my wife calls him, "The best Hach that ever hached") has the beginning of a bad back.

After I feed him, he toddles back to the bed, now lying with his head on my pillow. I guess he likes the smell and that still-warm part of the bed.

I check my email quickly because I don't want him to have to cross his legs, and we go on our morning hike, with me sensitive to when he needs to stop to pee or poop. Lest you think I'm a total wimp, I'm aware that experts say that you and not the dog should decide when and where to stop. I usually do but am not averse to his occasionally pulling me where he especially would like to bestow his unholy water.

We end up at my favorite cafe, a 15-minute hike from home, at which point in violation of the (silly) California Health Department rule against sweet, flea-free doggies, all the baristas welcome my Hach. I attach his leash to my chair whereupon he takes a nap but is gladly interrupted when people ask if it's okay to pet him. I gush, "Absolutely" whereupon Hachi usually looks up and, on being petted, rolls over and paws for a belly rub.

At this point, I want to additionally validate that Hachi is the world's sweetest dog by mentioning that he has barked only twice in his six-year life, each time inexplicably and just for a moment. I love my Hachi but as a security guard, he gets an F — He'd roll over for a belly rub. He didn't even bark when I had inadvertently closed the door upon returning from the deck and didn't realize he was still outside. Three hours later I realized it and there he was, napping in a shady spot, peaceful in the knowledge I'd eventually retrieve him.

When we get back from our morning constitutional, I go to my desk whereupon, you guessed it, he takes a nap on the dog bed I've attached to the ottoman next to my desk. When I crave a bit of dog love, I just lean over, give him a little love and he typically makes a noise that's the canine equivalent of a purr.

Own work

In recent years, most of my clients are by phone or Zoom, but when I have an in-person client, Hachi typically lies on the sofa next to my client. Many clients spend part of the session petting him while talking. Indeed, I've printed up the business card shown above:

In the evening, my wife and I get pleasure from giving Hachi treats, more belly rubs, and from his nuzzling between us as we watch TV. Come bedtime, he jumps on the bed, I kiss him goodnight, and he settles in for a good night's sleep next to my leg.

People assume that because I work long hours discretionarily, I must love my work. No, I work because I want to spend lots of time using my abilities constructively. But love? That's pretty much restricted to my wife and, yes, my sweet, sweet, Hachi.

Hachi, My Co-Counselor

To be accurate, Hachi is my receptionist, co-counselor, stress management consultant, and fitness trainer. He greets my clients with an enthusiasm no paid receptionist could match. I mean, even if I paid a receptionist $100,000 a year, s/he wouldn't give each client a sloppy kiss. Hachi recognizes that he has another job. So he escorts the client to the sofa, of course, sitting next to him, perhaps bestowing another round of kisses.

The author and his previous dog,

Of course, there is the occasional client who prefers career counseling without a face washing. In those cases, undeterred,

Hachi assumes the position: head on the client's shoes.

Jack of all trades, master of all, Hachi is my co-counselor. Even though I'm a career counselor not a psychotherapist, sometimes a client gets anxious during a session. So when clients feel stressed, they often pet Hachi and if they were already petting him, they tend to speed up—a useful anxiety detector for me.

Hachi wears two other hats. He is my stress management consultant, on call 24/7. When stressed, I often snuggle up to him on the floor, nose to nose, and rub his belly. 30 seconds of that evaporates anxiety.

Hachi is also my fitness trainer. Without him, it's tempting to sit on my butt but Hach needs his exercise and poopertunities, so we take walks four times a day, one a vigorous 45-minute hike. An overpriced, overmuscled fitness trainer couldn't keep me that diligent.

Like many dog owners, Hachi is a beloved family member. I'm embarrassed to admit it but I care about my doggie more than I do most people. I love him almost as much as my wife. He's a true member of the family, even if he weren't the world's best receptionist, co-counselor, stress reducer, and fitness trainer.

Thoughts I'd Share Mainly with My Dog

Hachi and me, own work

I am scared of aging and it fuels in me, **the urgency of the aged.** For some people that's to play a lot: travel, golf, grandkids, spending. For me, it's to work long hours — writing, seeing clients, giving talks on my books. Honestly, I look down on people who fritter that most valuable of possessions: time.

I do like simple pleasures that take little time: coffee while working, petting my dog, listening to an audiobook while driving.

I am sad that for all the writing I've done, I feel I've made too little difference. I believe I've helped my clients but my writing, less so. You see, except for this book, I've focused on writing on things I believe but aren't part of the standard thinking — To write in support of conventional wisdom, au courant thinking, would make my writings mere grains of sand on a beach. Perhaps because of that, I believe I haven't moved the needle at all. Yet, I continue to write. I don't do it because I enjoy writing. I don't — It's work. I write because I think I do it well, have some followers, and yes, I hold the likely vain hope that my ideas — especially my valorizing of merit over DEI (diversity, equity, and inclusion) — will sooner or later be recognized as wisdom. Perhaps I should just shrug at my perceived lack of impact.

POEMS

Dog Walker

Ruldoph Furtado, Wikimedia, CC 0

Dog walkers,
those sweet rejects
to canine care
relegated:

primped pup
foster care.

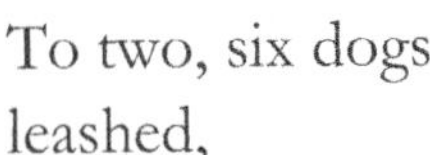

To two, six dogs
leashed,

pulling you, kissing you.

A deal that's okay except the pay.

Sad that the world hires you only this way.

A Piggy Dog Walker

Roger Cornfoot, Geograph, CC

Silly me thinks that a
friend worthy of me

will see that my
gardened jeans

judge me keen

not its gift-wrap mean.

So oft my doggie I lead

with knees clayed and weedy

plus my hair Einsteinian indeed,

hoping to see a face with a seed of interest

agreed to be of mutual need.

But I always return home

just with a dog who peed.

A Puppy Within

From rejection and the worry,

my face reads stern:

gullied brow, barren head, mouth corners down,

own work

the sum of life's infection.

But beneath my visage foreboding

lies faint still hoping

for acceptance and belly rubs.

A FINAL NOTE

People often ask how busy people like my wife and I have time for a dog.

Yes, it is time-consuming. It's like caring for a baby who never grows up.

My wife, Hachi, and me. Own work

But perhaps especially because we're so busy—and if I'm to be honest—I'm prone to be stressed—sweet Hachi is well worth the time.

It's not just the unconditional love, although there's that, it's the reliable, comforting rituals— from his lifting his head when we wake up and toddling over to snuggle, to the daily walk where we hang out at a café, to the last pet at night, which I always end with, "Good night, sweet Hachi."

Consider adopting from a shelter: Most shelter dogs are mutts, so you get the health benefit of hybrid vigor, they're dramatically less expensive than purebreds, and yes, you may well save a life. Check out sites that aggregate shelter pets from across many rescue facilities such as, PetFinder.com, AdoptaPet.com, and PetSmartCharities.org

As I mentioned at the beginning of this book, I welcome your emailing me to let me know what you think of it. I promise to respond. My email address is mnemko@comcast.net.

Marty Nemko

Made in the USA
Coppell, TX
31 July 2024

35422731R00066